PUFFIN BOOKS

GRIMBLE

Grimble was a fairly ordinary boy of about ten with unusual parents . . . who were in their middle thirties.

While Grimble was decently organized his parents were vague, unreliable, unpredictable, and seldom got things completely right.

Sometimes this was a good thing . . . like when it came to bedtime and no-one remembered, but there were disadvantages.

For instance, one day when he came home from school, there were notes to say they had gone to Peru, also notes about brushing his teeth and stopping the milk (his parents were good at notes). The old Grimbles did provide a list of people to whom Grimble could go for cook-yourself meals, and as nothing was said about washing up, he left the washing up.

Also there was Christmas, which Grimble was very much afraid his parents had forgotten, in spite of the fact that he went round the house humming carols and dropping pine needles . . .

The Grimble family is a refreshingly funny and original creation which started life on BBC TV's Jackanory. The author, Clement Freud, journalist and food writer, says he wrote the books because his children bullied him into them.

For readers of eight and over; also for mothers and fathers interested in washing up.

Clement Freud was born in 1924, the son of an architect, grandson of the psychoanalyst. He trained as a chef at the Dorchester Hotel in London, before joining the Ulster Rifles in 1943. He finished the war as a Liaison Officer in Nuremberg at the war crimes trials. He began writing after the war and is perhaps the first and last journalist to write simultaneously for three different national papers. He was for several years a Liberal M.P. He is married with five children, and lives in London, Suffolk and the Hebrides.

D1421640

GRIMBLE

AND

GRIMBLE AT CHRISTMAS

Clement Freud

Illustrated by Quentin Blake

PUFFIN BOOKS

PUFFIN BOOKS

Published by the Penguin Group
27 Wrights Lane, London W8 5TZ, England
Viking Penguin Inc., 40 West 23rd Street, New York, New York 10010, USA
Penguin Books Australia Ltd, Ringwood, Victoria, Australia
Penguin Books Canada Ltd, 2801 John Street, Markham, Ontario, Canada L3R 1B4
Penguin Books (NZ) Ltd, 182–190 Wairau Road, Auckland 10, New Zealand

Penguin Books Ltd, Registered Offices: Harmondsworth, Middlesex, England

The first story, *Grimble*, first published by Collins 1968
The second story, *Grimble at Christmas*, first published in Puffin Books 1974
Published in Puffin Books 1974
9 10

Set, printed and bound in Great Britain by
Cox & Wyman Ltd, Reading
Set in Monotype Imprint

Contents

Part 1

GRIMBLE

1. Monday

THIS is a story about a boy called Grimble who was about ten. You may think it is silly to say someone is *about* ten, but Grimble had rather odd parents who were very vague and seldom got anything completely right.

For instance, he did not have his birthday on a fixed day like other children: every now and then his father and mother would buy a cake, put some candles on top of it, and say, 'Congratulations Grimble. Today you are about seven', or, 'Yesterday you were about eight and a half but the cake shop was closed.' Of course there were disadvantages to having parents like that – like being called Grimble which made everyone say, 'What is your real name?' and he had to say, 'My real name is Grimble.'

Grimble's father was something to do with going away, and his mother was a housewife by profession who liked to be with her husband whenever possible. Grimble went to school. Usually, when he left home in the morning, his parents were still asleep and there would be a note at the bottom of the stairs saying, ENCLOSED PLEASE FIND TEN P. FOR YOUR BREAKFAST. As 10p is not very nourishing he used to take the money to a shop and get a glass of ginger beer, some broken pieces of meringue and a slice of streaky bacon. And at school he got lunch; that was the orderly part of his life. Shepherd's pie or sausages and mashed potatoes on Monday, Tuesday, Wednesday, Thursday; and on Fridays, fishfingers. This was followed by chocolate spodge – which is a mixture between chocolate sponge and chocolate sludge, and does not taste of anything very much except custard – which the school cook poured over everything.

One Monday Grimble came back from school, opened the door and shouted, 'I am home.' No one shouted anything in answer. So he went round the house looking for messages because his parents always left messages. It was the one thing they were really good at.

On a table in the sitting-room there was a globe. And stuck into the globe were two pins each with a triangle of paper on it. One of these was stuck into England and said GRIMBLE, and the other was stuck into Peru and said US. He went into the kitchen and here was another note: TEA IS IN THE FRIDGE, SANDWICHES IN THE OVEN. HAVE A GOOD TIME.

In the bedroom was a note saying YOU WILL DO YOUR HOMEWORK, WON'T YOU? P.S. DON'T FORGET TO SAY YOUR PRAYERS.

In the bathroom a message TEETH.

He walked round the house thinking they've really been very good, and then he went to the back-door and saw a note MILKMAN. NO MILK FOR FIVE DAYS.

He changed the note to NOT MUCH milk for five days, and sat down in the kitchen and started to think about things. Five days is a long time for any-one and an especially long time for a boy of ten who is never quite sure whether he might not be missing his birthday. It had been weeks since he last had a birthday. He got a piece of paper and worked out five days at twenty-four hours a day and made it over a hundred hours, actually a hundred and some-thing hours. He decided to have a sandwich. He opened the oven door, found the oven absolutely full of sandwiches, and took one with corned beef and apricot jam in it. It was a bit stale, like sand-wiches are when they have been made a long time ago, so he lit the oven to freshen the sandwiches up a bit and decided to write a poem about his situation. This is what he wrote:

> My Situation
> by Grimble
> When parents go to Peru
> And leave cups of tea in the fridge,
> It's jolly hard to know what to do
> And I wish I could think of a useful
>   word ending in idge.
> The End

It was not a very good poem and it hadn't even taken very long to write, so he opened the door of the refrigerator and found bottles and bottles of tea. He poured himself a cup and sipped it. The tea did not taste very nice and it was not very hot, so he took his football out into the yard and kicked penalties with his left foot. As a matter of fact Grimble could not kick the ball at all with his right foot, but very few people knew this, so when he had friends whom he wanted to impress he used to say, 'Come and see me kick penalties with my left foot.' It worked very well.

After scoring one hundred and seven goals he went back to get a proper fresh sandwich. He opened the oven door and a very sad sight met his eyes. The sandwiches had been wrapped in pieces of paper, and the oven had burnt the paper, and all the butter had run out on to the bottom shelf, and the fillings of sandwich-spread and peanut butter and honey and lemon curd and cheese and pickles were sizzling in the butter. He got a teaspoon, tasted some of the mixture, and decided he preferred Weetabix, but as he was tasting it his eyes fell upon another note stuck on to the oven door and only a little bit brown from the heat of the roast sandwiches.

IN CASE OF EMERGENCY said the note GO TO and there followed a list of five names and addresses all of them very near Grimble's house. He felt much better, kicked two more goals and went off to the house of the first name on the list.

MR WILFRED MOSQUITO 29 BACK STREET (RING TWICE).

Back Street was just round the corner from his house, so he ran over there, and on the front door he found a note which said WELCOME GRIMBLE, THE KEY IS IN THE MILK BOTTLE. He opened the door, went in and found another note: FOOD IS IN THE KITCHEN. KITCHEN IS BEHIND DOOR MARKED KITCHEN, and in the kitchen there was a big piece of paper which said: HELP YOURSELF.

The Mosquitoes' kitchen was big and bright, and there was a vegetable rack with coconuts and bananas and limes in it – limes are like lemons, only green – and a bottle of rum stood on the shelf, and the 'fridge had a lot of meat in it, all raw. He tried a

sip of rum and did not like it much. It was strong. So he ate a banana and tried to kick a left-footed penalty with a coconut against the kitchen door, but a big chip of paint came off and he thought, I am a guest and I am not even supposed to chip paint off the doors in my own house; so he stuck the paint back on to the door again using the sludge on the inside of the banana skin as sticky paste, and went on an exploration of the house.

As far as he could see the Mosquitoes were a man and a woman and one child with a lot of clothes (or possibly three children with not very many clothes each), also six cats. He was sure about the six cats because he found them in a basket under the stairs. They had a saucer of milk and another saucer of meat that smelt a bit of fish. There were a lot of photographs of people in the sitting room and all the people in them were black. There was also a map of Jamaica. Grimble, who did not like to jump to conclusions but when it came to being a detective was every bit as good as Old Sexton B. and Sherlock H. and Dixon of Dock G., decided that the Mosquitoes were Jamaicans.

He decided this especially when he found a newspaper called the *Daily Gleaner*, printed in Kingston, Jamaica. Reading the paper he noticed on the front page a message telling you to turn to page seven for this week's recipe, *Coconut Tart*.

He turned to page seven.

Coconut tart, wrote the good woman who had thought of the recipe, *can be made by a child of eight*.

As Grimble was older than eight he realized that he would be able to achieve a coconut tart with great ease, took the *Daily Gleaner* into the kitchen, propped it up against the coconut, and started to read the instructions.

Make a short pastry in the usual way, it began. Grimble thought this an exceedingly stupid remark and was pleased to see that the writer must have realized this also because she continued, *by taking half a pound of flour, quarter of a pound of fat, half a teaspoon of salt and two tablespoons of water. Or you can use one of those ready-made tart-cases.* 'Why didn't you say so at the beginning, you stupid book!' said Grimble, and went out into the Mosquitoes' garden to try and catch a fat pigeon. The fourth time he threw his jacket over the fat pigeon's head, it gave him a sad tired look, waddled off and flew away.

Grimble went back into the kitchen.

For the filling, said the recipe in the paper, *you will need half a pound of grated coconut, a tablespoon of warm golden syrup, and two beaten eggs.*

He beat two eggs, and started to look for the coconut. It had gone. He remembered seeing it in the vegetable rack; he remembered kicking it, he remembered that very well because he still had a pain in his left foot. He read several pages of the *Daily Gleaner* to see if perhaps they said how one could make a coconut tart without a coconut, but all he found were pages and pages of small print headed *Work Wanted* and *Cars for Sale*, and it was not until he got to the last page that he found the coconut. It was propping up the paper.

Grimble like most small boys thought that a coconut grew on a piece of metal in a fairground, and did not know how one turned the hard brown hairy thing that never moved when you threw wooden balls at it into fluffy white coconut meat that you got in a chocolate coconut bar. He might never have found out if he had not decided to have one more left-footed penalty, using the kitchen table as the goal. The coconut hit the goalpost (actually the leg of the table), and broke in half. As it did so, a large puddle of white coconut milk seeped across the kitchen floor.

This was quite a helpful thing to happen. First of all it showed him where the fluffy white meat was, and secondly he had begun to feel he ought to do something about the six cats under the stairs, and now there was all this milk. He decided that six cats was much easier than a cloth and a bucket.

Grating a coconut is not as easy as it looks because

the flesh grows on the inside of the shell and it means wedging it off before you can get at it. Also the grater had a big notice tied to it which read

GRIMBLE, MIND YOUR FINGERS, so it was a slow business. But in the end it all worked, and he put the egg and syrup and coconut into the tart-case, and baked it the way they said, and shooed the cats out of the kitchen, and when the tart was cooked he ate it almost immediately. It was the best thing he had eaten since the corned beef and apricot jam sandwich.

When he had finished it was seven-fifteen, and

as his official bed-time was seven-thirty, he went home. When he opened the door he saw a telegram on the mat. It was addressed to him. He opened it carefully and read the message: SENDING TELE-GRAM TOMORROW. LOVE FATHER AND MOTHER.

Just before he went to bed he wondered why they had not sent the message they were going to send tomorrow in today's telegram, but he got so mixed up trying to work it out that he brushed his teeth, said his prayers and fell asleep.

2. Tuesday

THE morning after Grimble had eaten his coconut tart, he woke up very early because one does not sleep very well on fresh coconut tart eaten hot from the oven. He rushed downstairs. On the mat he saw another telegram, addressed to him with the word *Priority* stamped on one corner. 'Priority' means very important, very urgent. He opened it carefully and read the message: GRIMBLE. TAKE NO NOTICE OF YESTERDAY'S TELEGRAM. LOVE FATHER AND MOTHER.

The telegram was difficult to understand, because the previous day Grimble had had a telegram saying sending telegram tomorrow, and today was tomorrow, and if his parents did not want him to take any notice of yesterday's telegram it meant that they would not send a telegram today but they had just sent one, and here it was in his hand now. It was very perplexing. He went down to his father's room and took another look at Peru which had the flag marked US sticking in it, and measured the distance from London to Lima, which is the main town in Peru. It was about the width of one of his hands and two fingers. He picked up the globe to take a closer look and underneath it he found another message.

GOOD MORNING, GRIMBLE, it said. HOPE YOU SLEPT WELL. BY THE TIME YOU READ THIS WE WILL BE SENDING YOU ANOTHER TELEGRAM WHICH SHOULD REACH YOU WHEN YOU COME BACK FROM SCHOOL. PLEASE REMEMBER TO WASH BEHIND YOUR EARS, DON'T DRINK YOUR MILK TOO QUICKLY OR IT MIGHT TURN INTO CHEESE, AND STOP USING THE FACE FLANNEL ON YOUR SHOES. YOU KNOW WHERE THE SHOE BRUSH IS.

Grimble's school was quite a long walk away from his house. If one arrived early one met a woman called Mrs Smug who cleaned the corridors and kept cough sweets in the pockets of her apron. She gave the cough sweets to the boys, because she did not like cough sweets but had a very nasty cough, and her doctor had said she must take six of them to work every day and come home without them.

'Good morning, Grimble,' said Mrs Smug, coughing very nastily. 'Would you like a cough sweet?'

As Grimble had just seen a spider climbing out of Mrs Smug's other pocket and hated cough sweets (and marzipan), but was a very polite boy, he said, 'I would prefer not but will if you insist. Actually I still feel a bit ill from last night's coconut tart.'

'That is as maybe,' said Mrs Smug, using one of her favourite phrases.

'Cooked the coconut tart myself,' Grimble added proudly.

'Good heavens,' said Mrs Smug, which was the favourite phrase of her late husband. 'You made a coconut tart all on your own?'

'With coconut,' said Grimble.

'Did you rub the flour into the fat?' asked Mrs Smug.

'I did exactly as it said I should in the paper,' said Grimble, and just then the school bell clanged and Grimble ran into the building.

The teacher was calling out the names of the boys to see who was there. He called out a name, and if no one answered he marked his sheet *d or a* which meant that the boy in question was either deaf or absent. If any boy's name was marked *d or a* for more than a week, he would send a doctor to the boy's house. The doctor always carried an ear syringe in case it turned out that the boy was deaf.

'Gamble?' said the teacher.

'Here sir,' said a boy.

'Glitter?'

'Sir,' said another.

'Green?'

There was a silence.

'Come on, Green,' said the teacher. 'Speak up boy, I can't hear you.'

As nothing happened and no one said anything,

the teacher marked him *d or a* and called out, 'Grimble'.

'Here sir,' said Grimble.

That morning they had history.

'I want,' said Mr Willow, the history master, 'you boys to write down the names of all the Kings and Queens of England while I sit down at my desk and watch you. There will be no talking, and the last boy to finish must stay behind after school and mend my bicycle pump.'

Five minutes later Mr Willow was asleep in his chair, and the boys were making paper darts out of their exercise books and floating them all over the class-room. When the bell rang for the end of the lesson Mr Willow woke up and said, 'There now; let that be a lesson to you. I hope you have learnt something. Battle of Waterloo 1815. Magna Carta 1215. Lunch 1.15.'

Lunch on a Tuesday was sausages and mash unless they had had sausages and mash on Monday, in which case it was shepherd's pie made from yesterday's cut up sausages, covered with old mashed potatoes.

None of the other boys were very keen on the food – which is probably why so many stayed away from school – but Grimble liked it very much. He liked everything about school because it was tidy and organized and he always knew what was going to happen next, which was a nice change from his life at home.

After lunch it was sport. The boys got into a coach and were taken to a playing field by the side of a wood where there was one goal at the top of a hill. Some of the older boys said that there used to be another at the other end of the field, but a few years ago on Guy Fawkes' night someone had tied a rocket to the goal post and the whole thing had shot up into the air and no one had known where it had come down.

As shops do not sell single goals, and his school was too sensible to buy two goals and be left with one for which they had no use, they played a game called Twinge. This was just like football except that for the first half eleven boys stood in goal and the other eleven shot the ball at them, and for the second half everybody changed sides. The team that scored more goals were called the winners and were allowed to go home without having to have a bath. As Grimble's side lost by 61 goals to 2, Mrs Turtle, the games mistress, kept them quite late and by the time he got back to his house the telegram had lain on his doormat for so long the edges were beginning to curl up. He opened the envelope and inspected the message: THINKING ABOUT YOU. MESSAGE IN THE IRONING CUPBOARD. DON'T FORGET TEETH. LOVE FATHER AND MOTHER.

That, decided Grimble, was more like a telegram. He went up to the ironing cupboard, rummaged about a bit among the clothes, and finally in the pocket of his bathing trunks he found the message. It was written in green ink on a large

squashed-fly biscuit and said, DO NOT EAT THIS
BISCUIT BECAUSE EATING GREEN INK IS BAD
FOR YOU. LOVE FATHER AND MOTHER. 'If that
is a grown-up joke I am glad I am a child,' thought
Grimble, brushed his teeth angrily, and looked at
the list of people his parents had told him to go and
see if he needed anything.

He quite liked the Mosquito household where he
had been yesterday, only by the time he had left the

kitchen had been absolutely full of washing-up – and washing-up (and marzipan), were two things he did not like. So he looked up the next people.

These were the Featherstones, who lived next-door in a house that had once belonged to a magician and was full of old silk hats and rabbits left behind from the old man's conjuring days. Colonel Featherstone was grey and fierce and was in charge of the army. When he had Field Marshals in for dinner and found that instead of a napkin his guests got eight silk handkerchiefs tied together with knots that no one could undo, he did not think this a bit funny. Mrs Featherstone was a kind lady who cooked muffins for her husband to try to make him happier, but Grimble did not think this worked very well. Sometimes when he was just going to sleep he could hear them arguing.

'I am sorry, dear,' said the Colonel's wife.

'Attention!' shouted the Colonel. 'Left turn, quick march, halt, about turn!'

It seemed a funny way to live.

When Grimble got to the front door he was pleased to see that they were expecting him.

GRIMBLE, said a notice tied to the stuffed parrot which served as a bellpull, COME ON IN. QUICK

MARCH. RIGHT TURN. HALT. SALUTE WHEN YOU SEE AN OFFICER.

Grimble came in and found himself saluting the gas cooker to which was fixed a note which said GRIMBLE, STAND AT EASE. EAT COLD MEAT AND SALAD. WELL DONE.

On the table was a leg of something that could have been an elephant but was probably beef. There was also lettuce and tomato and cucumber and beetroot and radishes and oil and vinegar and salt and lemon juice.

On a shelf was a box of eggs, and a book which was called *Army Manual About Eggs*.

He propped the book against one of the lettuces and began to read:

Attention, said the first sentence. *This is an egg.*

LESSON ONE: *Is It a Hard-Boiled Egg?* Grimble looked at the egg and said 'I don't know.' *Well then*, said the book, *spin it the way you would spin a top, and if it stands up it is boiled. If it squelches around slowly it means the yolk is galumping about inside the shell and it is raw.*

He turned the eggs and worked out which were raw and which were boiled.

LESSON TWO: *Open the eggs and see if you were right.* This was going to be fun. He took the piles of raw eggs and hard-boiled eggs, and saw how many mistakes he had made.

LESSON THREE: *How to Make a Halved Hard-Boiled Egg. Take knife in right hand. Hold egg with left hand. Push down knife.*

LESSON FOUR: *How to Make Salad Cream called Mayonnaise.*

Having made the mayonnaise he dipped the hard-boiled egg halves into it and ate them. As there were lots and lots of pages of the manual still

to read he decided to look to the end of the book because usually, if you turn to the last page, you get the best part.

He turned to the last page and it said, *Grimble. Attention. Wipe your mouth. Go to bed.*

He stood up, saluted smartly, and left Colonel Featherstone's house.

When he got home he brushed his teeth, said his prayers and was just going to sleep when he remembered his homework: it was to write a poem about a horse. So he got a piece of paper and wrote:

> The Horse
> by Grimble
> A horse has got more legs than I
> But fewer than a centipede,
> He wears a bridle instead of a tie
> And is sometimes called a steed.
> The End.

Then he went to sleep.

3. Wednesday

WEDNESDAYS were Grimble's favourite days. When his parents were home his father used to say, 'Monday is not much fun because it is the beginning of the week, and you can't start anything on Fridays because there is no time left in which to finish it, but Wednesday is about right.' On Wednesdays Grimble used to get up early and get fresh hot rolls from the baker's shop; then he and his father cooked bacon and made scrambled eggs on toast and had fizzy lemonade.

After that they would look at the newspapers.

His father read out the headlines and Grimble would try to guess the next line.

'Small war in Penguin Island,' read his father.

'One penguin slightly hurt,' said Grimble.

'Crystal Palace Football Club beats Leeds United,' said father.

'Crystal Palace manager faints,' said Grimble.

'"I lied," said politician,' said his father.

'That can't be a *head*line,' said Grimble; 'it is much too every day.'

After that Grimble would go to school and his father would go back to bed, 'keeping myself for something important', he used to say. Once when Grimble came back from school his father was still in bed fast asleep. Grimble decided it must be something very important for which he was keeping himself.

As Grimble woke up on this Wednesday he had just begun to feel, 'Oh good, it's Wednesday,' when he remembered it was not so good – because his parents were still in Peru and it would be no fun eating hot rolls on his own, also he did not know how to cook bacon. There *were* a few bottles of fizzy lemonade in a cupboard but he only drank fizzy lemonade to please his father. Grimble very much preferred black coffee without sugar.

He got up and dressed and found the cake tin with money in it in the oven, took two coins and bought two white chocolate bars. He munched them on the way to school making sure that he did not arrive too early and get caught by Mrs Smug.

After he had answered his name at roll-call he went into the classroom for geography. He liked geography very much and was specially interested in it at the moment, because he thought he might learn something about Peru, but Mr Tottenbrough, the geography teacher, said, 'Good morning boys, today I am going to teach about Birmingham.' Grimble said, 'Good morning, sir, do you think you could teach us about Peru instead?' but Mr Tottenbrough said : 'Quiet boy. I never teach South American countries on Wednesdays. You should know that. Take twenty lines.' Twenty lines meant that Grimble had to write out: *Mr Tottenbrough never teaches South American countries on Wednesdays* twenty times.

He was then taught all about Birmingham for an hour and a half, multiplied things and divided other things for an hour and a half, and ate sausages and mash, and chocolate spodge for forty-five minutes.

In the afternoon they went to the swimming pool. The pool was new and belonged to some people called the Council who were always sending notes to Grimble's school asking boys not to make so much noise, to slop less water about and to try to remember other people who wanted to swim. Saturday was sports day, and Grimble's school had to choose teams for the different swimming events. Grimble was quite good at the under-eleven butterfly stroke but as they only wanted six boys in the final and there were seven under-eleven butterfly-strokers, they had a race to see who would be last

and not swim on Saturday. The seven boys got into the bath at the deep end, a man said ready, steady, go, and the boy next to Grimble, who was called Blatt, did a very big deep butterfly stroke, came up with several mouthfuls of water, banged his head against the rail, and sank.

As Grimble realized that there was now no point in using up a lot of energy in *not* coming last of seven when there were only six swimmers he swam very slowly and came last of six.

'The following boys will swim in the final on Saturday,' shouted the swimming master, and he read out five names and Grimble's.

When he got home that afternoon he looked for a piece of paper and wrote out a telegram. GRIMBLE PERU. AM IN UNDERELEVEN BUTTERFLY-STROKE FINAL SATURDAY IMPORTANT YOU ATTEND LOVE GRIMBLE.

As telegrams cost so much for every word sent, he looked at his message and decided that 'under-eleven' was not very important to the meaning and might as well be taken out. Then there were the words 'am' and 'in'. If he wrote 'butterflystroke final Saturday' they would get the general idea. So he changed the piece of paper to: GRIMBLE PERU. BUTTERFLYSTROKE FINAL SATURDAY LOVE GRIMBLE and took it to the Post Office with his tin of money and they said, 'You can have some extra words because the least you can pay for a telegram to Peru is 75p.' So he took back the paper and wrote PLEASE COME BACK SOON BECAUSE I AM MISSING YOU A LOT LOVE GRIMBLE.

Then he went back home to look up the next name on the list which his parents had left for him. It would be nice, he thought, if one of the families were in when I arrived for dinner.

The third name on the list was Grimble's Aunt Percy. This, you may think, is an odd name for an aunt, but Percy's real name was Persimmon and she had always been called Percy from the time she was a child, and there seemed no good reason why she should change it now she was a middle-aged aunt. Aunt Percy lived in a flat which was so like all the other flats in the building that the only way you could tell hers was by the colour of the front door.

At the beginning, when the flats were first built Aunt Percy's door had been buff – which is really a non-colour like brown left out in the wind and the rain – and all the other flats had chosen colours like red and bright blue and pale yellow and green.

The trouble was that now, a few years after the flats had been built and left out in the wind and rain, all the other doors were about the colour that Aunt Percy had chosen in the first place.

So the people in the flats had a meeting and decided that everyone should write on the outside of each door the names of the people who lived on the inside of it. Aunt Percy was very angry about this. She said, 'I was the only one to choose a colour which you have now copied, and it's your own fault if no one can find you. I am certainly not going to write my name on my door. All my friends know that I live behind the buff door.'

The other people in the flats said that Aunt Percy was quite right; and now, as well as having their names on their buff doors, they also had the message *and Aunt Percy does not live here*.

So Aunt Percy had the flat with nothing written on it at all. Grimble walked past all the doors with names on them and finally came to the blank one and gave a shy knock, and as no one answered he pushed at it and it opened quite easily.

Of course all the flats were alike, and the only way Grimble could be sure it was his aunt's flat was to go into the bedroom and see that the carpet and the curtains and the sheets were buff-coloured.

He looked, and they were.

What was more, on a buff-coloured pillow case was pinned a note: WELCOME GRIMBLE. I HAVE HAD TO POP OUT FOR ABOUT A WEEK FOR SOME FISH FOR THE CAT. THERE ARE POTATOES AND A KNIFE IN THE KITCHEN, ALSO SOME QUITE ACCEPTABLE MILK WHICH I GOT IN 1972.

In the kitchen Grimble found the potatoes in a brown paper bag and propped the buff-coloured cookery book against them, and started to read.

The cookery book was written by a woman and was full of very boring womanish writing:

Hello Grimble, dear, it said on the first page, *I do hope you will love this little cookery book which I wrote all by myself specially with you in mind. If you are sitting comfortably with your little legs tucked under your little chair I want you to read everything very carefully, and then you will be able to make lovely potato things, won't you?* Grimble turned over the page and got to Chapter Two. *Boiling potatoes*, the boring woman had written, *takes about twenty minutes because potatoes are quite big and it takes the dear boiling water all that time to magic the inside soft.*

Grimble did not actually snort because he was too polite, but he gritted his teeth and picked up a potato.

'Now you dear little potato,' he said, 'if it takes twenty minutes to magic you soft in boiling water, why don't we . . .' and he whipped a knife out of a drawer, cut the potato in half and said, 'Now you dear little pot- and you dear little -ato you will each only take ten minutes.'

39

So he thought about it some more and cut the half potato in half again and said, 'Five minutes,' and then in half again and said, 'Two and a half minutes,' and then in half again and said, 'A minute and a quarter.'

He put some water on to the stove and when it was boiling he put in the piece of potato, timed it on the second hand of his watch, and after a minute and a quarter he took out the potato and it wasn't at all properly cooked.

He decided to give the woman another chance, turned to the middle of the cookery book and read a recipe for potato pancakes.

First of all, dear Grimble, he read, *I am terribly sorry about your boiled potatoes . . . oh, silly me. I do hope we shall be luckier this time. You need a potato, some milk, some flour, a little fat and an egg . . .*

It was a jolly good potato pancake even with the 1972 milk, and he sat down at the buff-coloured table and ate it up using a fork that had four prongs at one end and a pencil at the other. He thought this was a very good idea, so when he had finished eating he turned the fork round and did his homework.

He had been told to write a poem on women, so he wrote:

Women
by Grimble

Men are easily the best people I know,
Men are sensible and intelligent and good looking.
Some of my very best friends are men – like my father
And I'm jolly glad I haven't got a sister.
The End

As he was still full of writing and his poems were never longer than about four lines he wrote a note to his Aunt Percy.

Dear Aunt,
   I made myself a potato pancake; thank you for doing the washing-up. I hope you get some good fish.
                              Love,
                              Grimble.

Then he went home to bed and dreamt about hot
roast peanuts.

4. Thursday

GRIMBLE never slept very well; before he learnt to read, he used to lie in bed and twist a piece of soft material round his fingers and make shapes with it. When he started to read, he used to wait until it got light, and when he was given a torch for Christmas and woke up in the night, he lit his torch and read under the bedclothes. He liked thick books about battles and wars best.

Grimble was going to write a book himself when he grew up, and it would be all about how children spent too much time in bed, and that it was a great waste to go to sleep when you could read about how Hannibal and Caesar fought, or that tanks don't have a steering wheel but have brakes on each side so that if you want to go to the left you pull at the left brake and the right side of the tank overtakes the left and you turn round.

When the clock pointed to eight o'clock on Thursday morning Grimble had hardly slept at all and was feeling disgruntled . . . which means something between all right and angry.

When his parents were home, he had once come into their bedroom and said, 'I am not very well,' and his father had said, 'You are definitely disgruntled and must stay at home.' He had sent a note to his school saying: GRIMBLE POORLY. SIGNED FATHER GRIMBLE.

As his father was away and it was really up to Grimble to take his own decisions, he decided that he was not well enough to go to school, and wrote a note. It was quite a short note, neatly written and said: IT IS MY OPINION THAT GRIMBLE IS NOT WELL ENOUGH TO GO TO SCHOOL.

He wrote a name under it, like grown-ups do, so that you could not read it. He put the note into an envelope, addressed it to the headmaster, and went off to deliver it. When he arrived at the gates of the school the master was just calling out the names and had got to Glum and Gray . . .

'Grimble,' he called out.

'Absent, sir,' said Grimble waving the letter at the man. But the master took no notice, went on reading the names, closed his book and went into the school. So Grimble put the envelope into his pocket and stayed at school. He thought it was most unfair. After a while he was quite glad that he had stayed at school because Miss Fishnet, the religious teacher,

44

was ill and they went into the playground and had a game of football, and he scored three goals, two of them with his left foot, and the other sort-of-with-his-knee. Football in the playground was a very good game because when you played you could see all the other boys sitting in their classrooms doing lessons.

In the afternoon they did French. Monsieur Boudin was the French master and he pronounced all the boys' names in French ... Grimble was Grimbell with a nasty rolling 'r'.

'*Alors Grimbell*,' said Monsieur Boudin, 'Speak French.'

'*Oui Monsieur,*' said Grimble because he had only started to learn this term and had not got much further than *Oui Monsieur* and *Non Monsieur*, which mean 'Yes sir' and 'No sir', and clearly *Oui Monsieur* was the better of his two sentences.

'What is French for a dog?' said Monsieur Boudin.

Grimble absolutely hated saying I don't know, so he said '*Un whoof*'. Monsieur Boudin was a bit deaf so he said, 'Again', and Grimble thinking he had almost got it right said, '*Un whoof whoof.*'

'*Chien,*' said the French master, 'write down *chien*, and while you are writing it down also write down *chat* which is "cat". Write it down very often, then I can have a little sleep.'

Grimble decided that when he grew up he might become a schoolmaster and sleep in the daytime, then he could read all night.

When he got home from school that evening there was a telegram lying on the doormat. This time the message was absolutely clear. It said: RETURNING HOME FRIDAY NIGHT. INFORM MILKMAN REMEMBER TEETH. He sat down and worked out that this meant one more supper tonight; breakfast, fishfingers, supper tomorrow, and then his parents would be home.

He went into the garden, shot forty-three left-footed penalties, and decided to make his bed. Making beds was a very unnecessary habit. To Grimble, in fact to almost any reasonable person, a

bed looks as well with a few sheets twisted around and a pillow or two on the floor as it does if it is all tucked in and done properly. Also it is much easier to get into a bed when it was last used for getting out of, but as grown-ups make a great deal of fuss about tidiness he made his bed about once a week. This was quite a good idea because he often found things in the bed that he had lost and really given up hope for – like his pyjama trousers, and once a pea-nut butter sandwich under his pillow which he had completely forgotten about, though he had thought the bed had smelt a bit funny.

When the bed was made he twisted the plasticine he had found in it to look like a sausage dog and went to see what was the next name on the list of people who would give him supper:

STATION-MASTER WHEELER AT THE STATION.

I don't think I have said before that Grimble's house was very near the railway and trains went past it making a lot of noise. The point is that when you live like that you get so used to the noise that you don't notice it, and one day, when there was a strike and no trains were running, Grimble had woken up with a start and said, 'What was that?'

His father had come in and said, 'It's nothing. Just no noise.' The station was at the end of the street and Mr Wheeler was in charge of it. There were two little shops on the station, one of them selling newspapers, and the other things to eat –

like old sausage rolls and sandwiches that were wrapped in bits of paper as if no one expected anyone to unwrap them. There was also a machine with a sign on it saying *Platform tickets 1p* and the *1p* had been crossed out and *2p* put in its place.

Grimble wondered why it was now more expensive to stand on a platform, which is all you are allowed to do with a platform ticket, and Mr Wheeler had explained that it was probably because you now had to wait longer for trains.

The station had a notice outside it which said THIS IS THE STATION. YOUR FRIENDLY STATION-MASTER IS CALLED MR WHEELER.

Unfortunately the friendly station-master was out. Grimble went to the machine, bought a platform ticket and looked everywhere. The waiting-room was empty. There was no one behind the window marked *Tickets*, and the paper shop and the old wrapped-up-sandwich shops were empty. There was a timetable pinned up against the wall and on this there was a note: GRIMBLE. HAVE GONE TO SEE A MAN ABOUT AN ENGINE. GO TO THE SIGNAL BOX. P.S. WELCOME.

The signal box was at the end of the platform and was full of levers, so the signal man could pull a lever and the train turned left or right or went straight on depending on where they were meant to go. In a corner of the signal box was a metal box full of food and a gas-ring and a saucepan. The box marked *Food* had a padlock and in the keyhole of the padlock there was a message saying: KEY IS UNDER BOX.

Grimble felt it was silly to hide the key in so obvious a place and then leave a note so that absolutely anybody could find it; but then the station was a very small station. Mr Wheeler was probably not a very clever man or he would have got a really big station like Birmingham.

When he opened the box there was a tin of corned beef and a tin of biscuits and a tin of chocolate and a tin of sugar. There was also a tin of sardines and a bag of flour and a bottle of some very strong smelling brown drink which was almost empty and had ONLY TO BE USED IN EMERGENCY written on the label.

As it was a very large bottle and there was very little drink left in it Grimble realized that there must have been a lot of emergencies. Also in the box was a book called *The Signalman's Manual*. Grimble sat down and started to read it. It was very boring and he decided that he would definitely not become a signalman when he grew up.

This brought him to supper. When he had got all the tins out and laid them in a line he realized there was something missing. Chocolate, sugar, corned beef, sardines, biscuits, flour. What was missing was something wet. Like sauce. When you eat corned beef you have tomato sauce. When you eat sardines . . . tomato sauce. Biscuits . . . well, tomato sauce . . . or any sort of sauce.

Grimble took out a piece of paper and worked out that what he could have for supper (and a man must have sauce with what he eats), could be either corned beef with sardine sauce or sardines with corned beef sauce, or, and this seemed a very much better idea . . . with chocolate sauce.

He opened *The Signalman's Manual* and looked under *C*, and it had a chapter on couplings, and one on coal for engines, and a long one on clockwork, and right at the bottom of the page there was a little heading *Chocolate Sauce*. He was really *very* lucky.

Chocolate sauce, said the book, *is delicious whichever way you make it, but chocolate and sugar and flour and water are a help*. Now by a very strange piece of good fortune, chocolate and sugar and flour and water were exactly what he had.

He put a whoosh of chocolate into the pan, tasted it and said, 'Yes, it quite definitely needs water to get it wet for sauce,' and as the water was very thin he decided flour would be good to get it thick, and as he liked things sweet he added sugar.

He put the saucepan on the fire and decided to do his homework. It was to write a letter to an uncle thanking him for sending 50p and telling him what he was going to do with the money.

Dear Uncle [he wrote],

It was good of you to send me 50p, for which I am grateful. I am going to change it and put 12½p into my bank, spend about 5p on things for me like sweets and decide about the rest of the money later. I like money and already have quite a lot. I hope your nasty cough is better thank you again.

Grimble.

By the time he had written that, something very odd had happened to the chocolate sauce. It was making spitting noises, and bubbles of sauce would burst and splash bits of lumps on to *The Signalman's Manual*. Grimble thought that this served it right because if it had said *stir the sauce* it would never have happened. What was happening to the chocolate sauce was that the bottom part was burnt and the top was not even very hot, because if you cook things and don't stir them this sort of thing goes on.

Actually Grimble thought burnt chocolate sauce

was quite nice. He tried a little with his sardines, and then some with the corned beef. Thinking about it he thought that it tasted best with the biscuits. As there was a lot of washing-up and wiping-up to do he remembered that he had promised his parents always to be in bed in good time, and as this was a good time he went home. Only one more day, and possibly tomorrow when he came home from school his parents would already be there waiting for him. It might even be his birthday.

5. Friday

ON Friday Grimble woke very early and went out to give the pigeons the last of the sandwiches from the oven; these were now very stale and tasted evil but pigeons not only have poor table manners, they are unfussy about what they eat. He gave the fattest pigeon a five-day-old apricot jam butty and stood behind a tree with his jacket ready to catch it. The pigeon waddled along, looked down at the curled up piece of bread, pecked at it, and at that moment Grimble dived. The pigeon took a quick step to one side and Grimble landed on the sandwich. He wiped the jam carefully from the inside of his jacket and decided to have breakfast out.

Yesterday's chocolate sauce had been very interesting but he felt like something special before the Friday fishfingers – he thought a bacon sandwich would be nice.

The shop on the corner which sold newspapers was so steadily empty that one could always get anything else one wanted done there. Grimble said, 'Good morning, could I have a button sewn on to my jacket, and a clean handkerchief, and a bacon sandwich while I read your newspaper?' The woman said, 'Of course, that's what I am here for,' and Grimble read *School holidays begin soon* in one paper and *School holidays have just begun* in another. Newspapers don't lie, his father had told him; they invent the truth.

As his school holidays began that afternoon, after school, he made a small note on his cuff about which newspaper told the truth and which one didn't, and read about football. His best club had lost the evening before and were bottom of the table. The woman in the paper shop came back with his jacket and the sandwich wrapped in a handkerchief. She was rather a silly woman; he blew his nose, ate the sandwich, gave the woman 5p, folded up the newspaper, saw that it now had a lot of very good bacon finger-prints on it, put it at the bottom of the pack, and went off to school.

The last day of term was a specially good day. Nothing that happens on the last day counts because the teachers have done the reports; if you have to stay in after school, you can't because school is finished. There were no real lessons, just teachers chatting and doing puzzles and telling the boys to clean out their desks and hand in their school books.

Next term they were all going up into another class except for Dashwood, Piercey and Trugg who were staying in the class for another term because Trugg couldn't count, Dashwood did not know the difference between reading and writing, and Piercey had had measles and had only been to school on the first day of term – and then again on the last day.

Grimble felt very very well all that morning, thinking about his parents flying back from Peru; when he got his milk at eleven he thought they would just about be passing Birmingham now. At lunch he thought they must be past New York, and when the bell went for end of school he decided that with the world going round one way and his parents coming another, they might have got back yesterday, only have been held up at the airport waiting for their luggage.

After school he ran straight home and shouted, 'I am here.' No one answered.

He went up to his parents' bedroom because when they had been travelling they sometimes went straight to bed; but the bed was empty and the note from the first day was still there. TEA IN THE FRIDGE, SANDWICHES IN THE OVEN. HAVE A GOOD TIME. Have a good time was a typical grownup remark that did not mean anything. He went to the 'fridge and took out the bottles of tea and poured them into the sink. His mother said tea was very good for children as it made the insides of their tummies golden-red-colour. Grimble did not mind what colour the inside of his tummy was; he did not like tea and as he drank quite a lot of coffee and ate white chocolate he thought his tummy was probably about the right colour anyway.

What would be especially nice, he thought, would be to get some sort of coming-home present for his parents. He went to the cake tin and it was still about one-third full of coins, so he took a handful and went to the shop on the corner, 'Good evening,' he said to the dotty lady. 'Could you give me a present for two people returning from Peru?'

The woman gave him a street map of Manchester and two pencils, and said, 'Would you like me to wrap them up?' Grimble said, 'Naturally. Whoever heard of a present that was unwrapped up?' So she wrapped the map and the pencils, and found a card which said *You are five today*. It was not terribly suitable but it was the only one in the shop, so he bought it and wrote *Welcome Home* on it and ran back to the house.

'I am home,' he shouted.

There was no reply.

He crept up the stairs and looked in the bedroom. Nothing. Just the HAVE A GOOD TIME note, so he went downstairs and looked at the list of names. The last name was MADAME BERYL'S CAKE-SHOP.

Madame Beryl was a friend of his mother who sometimes called and talked to her about self-raising flour and currant loaves. She was a very fat lady who smelt of vanilla essence. Grimble had once gone into the bathroom and found Madame Beryl standing on the scales and the pointer on the scales pointed to *Jones and Co.*, which is just after *16 stones*, all the way round from *1 stone*.

Madame Beryl's shop was past the station; there was a row of shops selling fish and children's clothes and electric light bulbs, and then the cake shop. On the shop window he saw a note which said BACK SOON, and under it she had written GRIMBLE, KEY TO THE DOOR IS IN THE FISH SHOP.

So he went into the fish shop and said, 'Please could I have Madame Beryl's key?' and the fish man said, 'Do you want chips with it?'

'Yes, please,' said Grimble, 'and a little wine vinegar on the chips. I don't care for malt vinegar very much. But I do like salt.'

He got a very large bag of hot chips and the key to the cake shop, and let himself into Madame Beryl's and ate chips. They were particularly well cooked chips, and when he had finished he wiped his fingers on the handkerchief and threw the chip paper into a waste paper basket in a corner of the shop (he missed the basket the first five times), and then went round exploring. The kitchen was at the back of the shop and when Grimble came into it he realized straightaway why the cake-shop woman was so fat. It was absolutely full of cakes and buns and rolls and fruit-loaves and meringues and macaroons and fairycakes and mince pies and fruit tarts. On the shelves there were packets of jelly and tins of fruit and bags of different kinds of sugars and jars of jams and treacles and syrups – and a mouse trap. There was also a note which said: GRIMBLE, PLEASE HELP YOURSELF. FRIDAYS ARE GOOD NIGHTS FOR TRIFLES. LOOK IN THE BOOK FOR INSTRUCTIONS.

He looked in the book under *T*. There were seven pages about tapioca and then a chapter on trifles.

'*This is a good thing to eat*,' said the book. '*My trifle is a mixture of fruit and cream and cake and jam and jelly and sugar and almonds and if you like custard, custard. It is eaten cold.*'

Grimble leaned the cookery book against the flower vase on the table and decided that a large bag of chips does not make people very hungry for trifle. But Madame Beryl had obviously gone to such a lot of trouble to get him all the things that go into a trifle that he felt he really should make it. After all it did not seem to be very difficult. He got some pieces of cake and poured on the juice from the peaches, and then put on some strawberries and a spoonful of jelly, and then a layer of custard, and then the cream, and then put some almonds into it. And then he thought, I could have put in the meringues and made it my own trifle . . . *trifle à la Grimble* . . . then I could write a cookery book and become rich and famous, and when I walked down the street people would point at me and say, 'There goes the inventor of *trifle à la Grimble*.' And others would say, 'Not *the* Grimble?' And the first lot of people would say, 'Yes, the Grimble of trifle fame.'

So he got a fish slice and lifted up some of the trifle, and put the meringue in the middle, and pressed it all into shape again, and put almonds into the holes his fingers had made, and it looked exceedingly handsome. As there were a lot of cake boxes about and the chips and vinegar were still doing their job in stopping him from being very hungry, he decided to take the trifle home. He might give it to his parents as a welcome-back present.

When he arrived at his house he opened the door and shouted, 'I am back.' There was no answer but there were about five suitcases in the hall which had not been there when he had gone out.

'I am back,' he shouted. 'Hello. Grimble calling parents over.'

No one answered.

He went up into the bedroom and there was no sign of them, though the note had gone. He came down again and looked in the front garden. No sign – and then he went into the kitchen. And there

they were, the three of them: his father and his mother and his trifle. Sitting very quietly at the kitchen table, and his trifle had been unwrapped, and stuck into the top of the cream were ten whole candles and one or two bits of candle, all alight.

'Peru's a bad place for cakes,' said his father. 'Never go there if you want cake. Really not.'

Grimble looked at his father and mother, and thought, they are back and school is over and tomorrow I shall get ten pence for breakfast and we'll read the newspaper together, and if they get up in time for lunch I might actually cook them something.

Part 2

GRIMBLE
AT CHRISTMAS

1. Seven Shopping Days
to Christmas

GRIMBLE'S parents were very forgetful. This was sometimes annoying, but having a forgetful father and mother also had advantages. For instance it meant that he had better bedtimes than most other children. Quite often he used to go into his father's room and say, 'I'm going to bed now; it's midnight'; and his father would say, 'Don't wait up for me' or 'Iquique is the only town I know with two qs!'

For most of the year Grimble – Grimble was his whole name, his parents had forgotten to give him any other names – rather enjoyed having a father and mother who were different from those of the other boys at school, but when it came to Christmas there were very definite disadvantages.

Grimble had only two more days of school before the Christmas holidays started – and the old Grimbles went around as if it were the middle of February or the end of August; anyway there was nothing special about the way they went around.

The shops in the High Street had windows decorated with lights and Father Christmases and wrapped-up packages and mince pies and a big notice saying ONLY SEVEN MORE SHOPPING DAYS TO CHRISTMAS on which the number of days before the twenty-fifth was changed every evening . . . it was very exciting.

And Grimble's mother went out with a big shopping bag – and came back with a cabbage, and one and a half pounds of cod fillets. I don't want to be unkind about cod fillets. They are perfectly all right but they just do not make you tingle all over. Anyway they didn't make Grimble tingle all over.

Grimble had a friend called David Sebastian Waghorn whose mother had said, 'We are going to have cold turkey on Boxing Day.' That is just about the same as saying, 'On Christmas Day, we are going to have hot roast turkey with stuffing and gravy and sausages and bacon and roast potatoes and brussels sprouts.' He waited anxiously for Mrs Grimble to give some small hint like that. The evening before she had said, 'Have you put the cat out?' and Grimble said, 'We haven't got a cat,' and Mrs Grimble said, 'Oh dear nor we have, don't forget to leave her a saucer of milk.'

Grimble watched his parents carefully for any

sign that they might have remembered why he was going to be on holiday and when, and what sort of treats he was going to get if he was going to get treats. He worked hard giving them well-mannered hints because it was terribly important to him that Christmas would be, well . . . complete.

One evening he dropped a lot of pine needles on the carpet . . . but as no one noticed or said anything and Grimble was very tidy, he got a dustpan and brush and swept them up again a couple of days later.

Also he tried to hum Good King Wenceslaus . . . mm mmmmmmmm mm mmmmmm m but he did not hum very well and his father thinking it was God Save The Queen, stood up and when Grimble had finished humming his father turned off the television set and went to bed.

So he practised humming some more. David Sebastian Waghorn had a joke about humming. 'Do you know why humming birds hum? Because they don't know the words.' Grimble thought David Sebastian Waghorn was a very funny boy.

The day before, Mr Grimble had come into the house with a large square parcel and Grimble, knowing that it was not polite to be openly curious, had gone into the kitchen and watched his father

take the parcel into the study through the slightly open door. It looked as if it might be a bicycle taken to pieces or a large box kite or possibly a new kind of cooker.

That evening his father said, 'Come into the study and see what I've got in my parcel. It's a foot-stool, I gave it to me . . .' and Grimble had clenched his teeth and said, 'Now you can lie back in your chair and don't even have to bend your legs.' His father was delighted that Grimble had got the point of the footstool so quickly and showed him where Iquique was on the globe of the world . . . it was about half-way down South America on the left-hand side.

'Do you expect to get anything else for Christmas . . . except for my presents . . .' he asked his father in an offhand way. 'A lot of weather,' said his father who had just found Birmingham on the globe.

That night when Grimble was in bed he started to think about Christmas very seriously. Christmas was a holiday and a time for eating interesting food and giving presents and receiving presents – some-one had told him that it was more blessed to do one than the other, but he kept forgetting which. Now the reason why children expected their parents to do things for them at Christmas was because parents are better organized than children and parents have more money than children.

In Grimble's case this was only partly true. His parents were not nearly as well organized as he; they kept forgetting to get up in the morning and sometimes forgot to go to bed for days on end and they never knew what time it was.

But the old Grimbles did have more money than he . . . or he hoped they did, because Grimble only had 19p and an Irish 5p piece. He lay in bed practising his humming and wondering whether, if one was really well organized, as he was – satchel packed; homework done; toothpaste squeezed out on to toothbrush; tie tied in a knot and opened out into a big loop so that it would go over his head; shoelaces done up so that he could step into his

shoes and wriggle them about till the heels gave way . . . anyway, if someone were really well organized, it should not be very difficult for him to make money . . . and if he had money then he could arrange the whole family Christmas celebrations.

One evening Grimble had listened to a television programme about money in which a man had said that the important thing was to find something that everyone needed. That way, you had a ready market for whatever you were going to sell . . . for instance the man explained: 'It is a better thing to go from house to house selling socks, which everyone wears, than suspenders – which are rubber straps that go round your leg below the knee and keep the socks up. Hardly anyone wears suspenders,' said the man. Grimble had never even heard of suspenders. 'Also,' said the man, 'you have to spend some of your money on getting people interested in your wares – this is called advertising.'

Grimble was very impressed and wrote a small note to remind himself: to sell successfully you have to find something everyone wants, and advertise it.

It was quite clear to Grimble that if a man wants to earn money by selling things, he would have to buy them first; the simple problem that Grimble had was what could he buy for 19p that he might be able to sell for a lot of money – because a turkey and a Christmas pudding and presents and everything would cost pounds. One of the masters at school had told them about an old Greek who was lying in a bathtub when an apple fell on his head and he shouted, 'Eureka, I've got it!' and invented gold, or something like that. Grimble lay in his bed thinking hard waiting to shout, 'Eureka, I've got it!' but he fell asleep.

In the morning he went to the shop on the corner and as it was empty he looked carefully around for something that everyone needed that cost 19p or less. There were rolls of flypaper and some suntan cream and washing soap and tins of sardines and lemonade crystals. These were all dusty, which is a bad sign. Suddenly he saw a loaf of bread and a great idea occurred to him: everyone needed bread; if he went around selling bread slice by slice to people so that they wouldn't have to go to shops he could become very rich. And then he thought most people already have bread, but if I sold toast ... not only sold it but took it to people just when they wanted it. When they were sitting at the breakfast table with butter on the knife and a marmalade jar in front of them ... the GRIMBLE HOME TOAST DELIVERY SERVICE. Proprietor Grimble. 'Eureka I've got it!' he shouted and the old lady came out from the back of the shop and said, 'If you've got it you'd better pay for it. That is the only way you can do things in a shop.'

Grimble was much too excited to explain, so he paid the lady 6p which was the price of that loaf of bread and went to school.

He didn't learn much at school that day because he was working out his toast business. The loaf of bread was in his locker; it was a cut loaf called THIN SLICED which seemed a silly name to give a loaf and it contained eighteen pieces of bread wrapped in greaseproof paper. (If the business really succeeds he thought, I might go into the greaseproof paper business.)

Every morning nearly everyone eats toast and, as toast is quite boring to make, Grimble decided that if he made toast at seven every morning and brought it to people all hot and ready they would definitely pay 2½p for three slices, which meant six times three slices in a loaf which is 15p back for 6p.

When he came home from school he sat down at his desk and got a large piece of paper and cut it in half and then cut each half into half again and then halved the four pieces of paper so that he had eight small pieces and on each one he wrote the message THE GRIMBLE HOME TOAST DELIVERY SERVICE PROPRIETOR GRIMBLE founded 1974. On the other side he wrote: Toast delivered, daily, tidily, un-burntly, punctually. 2½p for three slices. Our representative will call tomorrow morning with a free slice and awaits the pleasure of your order.

He took the eight pieces of paper and put four of them through the letter boxes of the four houses up the hill from his house and posted the other four through the doors on the downhill side. As he was going back home he decided that as he did not know a great deal about toast he had better go and see Madame Beryl, who was a fat kind friend of his mother's who kept a bakery shop and knew a lot about things like that.

'Good afternoon,' said Grimble, entering the shop. 'I would like to have a small discussion with you about bread.' 'I prefer,' said Madame Beryl, 'to talk about cake.' 'I meant to say toast,' said Grimble. 'I still meant cake,' said Madame Beryl. She eased her right foot out of her shoe, which came away with a small sigh of relief, and said, 'I would very much like to talk to you about bread AND toast but unfortunately I have to go and see a man about a wedding breakfast. Can it wait until after Christmas?'

'I am afraid,' said Grimble, 'that after Christmas will be exactly too late.' There was a small silence. 'I have done a very silly thing,' said Madame Beryl. 'I baked a cake which had not been ordered and now I don't know what to do with it and the dustbin is full. Do you think you would be very kind and take possession of it?' 'Oh, yes, thank you,' said Grimble, 'if it is really in your way.' And Madame Beryl put her foot back into her protesting shoe, got a quite large cake, gave it to Grimble, said, 'Oh dear, I must fly,' and started moving into the street like a cabin trunk. 'About toast,' said Grimble following her. 'Not toast,' puffed Madame Beryl. 'Never toast cake. Ice it with icing sugar and egg white,' and she waddled onto a bus.

Grimble found himself alone with a cake and then he thought, actually a cake with icing is a very Christmassy thing to have and tomorrow I shall start up my business and in nine days' time it will be Christmas Eve and even if my parents have forgotten, it's going to be an absolutely complete proper well organized Christmas.

2. Home Toast Delivery

THE next morning Grimble woke early. He had not slept very well owing to his business problems. His assets, with Christmas Eve eight days away, were one iced cake hidden in a cupboard, 13p in a money box, the Irish 5p piece and a wrapped loaf of which he had reckoned to give away eight slices in the cause of advertising.

The old Grimbles had a toaster with two slots in it and the idea was that you put in two slices of bread . . . and after a minute and a bit they would pop up, done to a turn.

What really happened was that after the allotted time the toaster gave a small whirring noise and a click and you had to get a knife or a fork or a spoon and prise out the bread which had got stuck. Looking at the situation calmly, Grimble realized that the toast industry was going to be something of a gamble until he had a full list of cash clients and was able to buy efficient machinery for the production of high-class wares.

The next morning he got up about seven o'clock,

took eight paper napkins and wrote on each of them, 'With the Compliments of G.H.T.D.S.' This meant the Grimble Home Toast Delivery Service; putting the initials was much quicker than writing out the words. He then counted out eight slices of bread, wrapped the remaining slices firmly in the grease-proof paper so that they would stay fresh, and decided to make the toast two slices at a time . . . because, being the first day he would have to stay and talk about money and delivery time. When things got organized he might be able to throw slices of toast straight through the letter boxes . . . provided the people did not have dogs or cats or mice.

At a quarter past seven he turned on the toaster, and put in two slices and as soon as they were ready he prised them out, wrapped them in the paper napkin and ran out of the house. He started at the two houses just up the hill from his; they were absolutely dark. No lights, nothing. He wondered whether there might be some money to be made out of The Grimble Reliable Morning Alarm Service – but decided that having invested so large a part of his capital in the toast business, he had better concentrate on that.

He went up to the first house and rang the bell; as nothing happened and the toast was certainly not getting any hotter he rang it again and knocked. After a while the lights in the house went on and a man opened the door.

'Good morning,' said Grimble. 'I bring you toast on behalf of the Grimble Home Toast Delivery Service. I expect you received my literature,' and he gave the man his best smile and the free slice of toast. The man looked at it with appreciation. It was well toasted toast. 'Oh yes,' said the man. 'G.H.T.D.S. come in.'

Grimble went into the house and the man said, 'Sit down. Good idea this toast delivery. The wife and I would like to join but we don't have breakfast. Can we use it for lunch?'

'I am afraid,' said Grimble, 'that as yet I have no lunch toast service, but if I may, I will enter your name and call again when such a service commences.'

He said good-bye and went to the next house. He rang the bell and waited and finally saw a man and a woman through the glass of the front door, the man with a walking stick and the woman, making little twitty whimpering noises, saying, 'Harold don't be so angry it might be the postman with a new 4p delivery that comes earlier than the 3p one . . . or possibly it is last week's 3½p letters come at last.'

'It's Grimble,' shouted Grimble through the letter box. 'the Grimble Toast Delivery Service.'

'Bless my boots,' said the man. 'It's the breakfast toast,' and he opened the door and asked Grimble to come in. 'Good morning Sir,' said Grimble. 'I do hope you received my letter.' The man said yes he had. 'Here,' said Grimble 'is your free slice of toast with the compliments of the directors of the company.'

The man unwrapped it and ate it quietly. 'Excellent,' he said. 'First class piece of toast. Congratulate you!' 'Thank you sir,' said Grimble. 'I'll take the service,' said the man. 'Three slices a day, eight o'clock prompt. Pay on Friday, start the day after Christmas. We're going away to shoot salmon in Scotland this afternoon. Nice to have met you.'

'After Christmas,' Grimble muttered. 'That's not going to help buy a turkey' – and he rushed home to make the next two slices, wondering why he was not feeling as happy as he had been earlier that morning. His parents were still asleep, the toaster was ready and in a very short time he had the new supply of toast and was at the house downhill from his own. As he went up the path a man opened the door and said, 'Aha come on in, been waiting for my toast,' and he took his free sample slice from Grimble's hand, buttered it, put marmalade on it and said, 'There.' Then he said, 'There,' two more times. Grimble wondered 'where' but decided that customers were always right, said nothing and waited. 'Good,' said the man. 'A bit too much butter but that may have been my fault. I'll take the service, every day . . . but I would prefer brown toast. All right?'

Brown toast. No toast. Toast after Christmas . . . Grimble said, 'Thank you, I shall let you know, at present the service is confined to white, thin, sliced which is the popular demand,' and went next door.

This time it was a woman who answered the door. Grimble preferred men. 'Hello,' said the woman, 'you've come about the toast.' Grimble admitted this. 'How old are you?' asked the woman. (This was really why Grimble preferred men.) 'About ten,' he said. 'Oh,' said the woman, 'how nice, I have a little nephew who is coming for Christmas. He is nine and three quarters, you must come and meet him.' There was a short silence. 'Excuse me,' said Grimble, 'how old are you?' The woman looked slightly put out and said, 'What an extraordinary thing for a small boy to ask.' Then she gave an embarrassed giggle and said, 'I-am-in-my-middle-thirties,' all in one gasp. 'How nice,' said Grimble, 'I have a mother at home who is in her middle thirties. I do hope you will be able to come round sometime and play with her. We live two houses up the hill. Now about the toast.' 'Ah yes,' said the woman, 'Toast. Actually we make our own toast.'

'I realize this,' said Grimble. 'But the point of the service is that we take the hard work out of toast for you at a very modest charge. 2½p for three slices.' The woman looked at Grimble and thought some more and finally said, 'May I sleep on it?' 'I would not advise it,' said Grimble. 'Sleeping on toast may well keep it warm but it would do nothing to keep it crisp and fresh.'

'I mean I would like to think about it tonight . . .' said the woman, and Grimble remembering his good manners said, 'Naturally Madam; our aim is to please,' and left the house.

When he got home his mother was up making toast with HIS bread. This was very unusual . . . I mean for his mother to be up was very unusual – and Grimble took four of the slices of toast his mother had made and, very quickly, because it was getting quite near his school time, he raced round the four remaining houses that he had warned of the toast service. He slipped the toast through the letter-boxes, shouted, 'Will try to come back this evening,' and ran home.

'Where have you been?' asked Mrs Grimble, her head inside the refrigerator. 'Out,' said Grimble, and realizing that this was not a very complete reply added, 'actually feeding under-privileged people.' His father had told him once that when people began a sentence with 'actually', it was nearly always a lie. His mother, who had not been listening, said, 'Here is your breakfast. Come home straight from school, because we are going shopping.'

'Shopping,' said Grimble; 'Christmas shopping and there are still six shopping days to go ...' 'Well,' said his mother, 'actually mostly going to the launderette and things.'

Grimble drank his glass of iced milk which his mother had finally taken out of the refrigerator and went to school. She said 'actually', said Grimble to himself. That means she was telling a lie. It is Christmas shopping.

Walking to school he thought about the eight slices of bread given away and the rest probably eaten by the old Grimbles. I don't know how anyone can make a living in this country. It's the fault of the Government. When I grow up I am going to be a Government. Then anyone with a good idea will be able to make a lot of money ...

That afternoon, when he returned from school, his father said, 'Some people called and left you some toast ... hold on I'll find it. I looked at it carefully and there are no messages in it. Just toast wrapped in a napkin with some initials on it ... I wonder what it can mean.' 'Actually,' said Grimble 'it's a new club' ... and blushed. It was the second lie he had told that day. His father went out and brought back three slices of toast still wrapped with the G.H.T.D.S. slip on them and just then his mother called, 'Come on Grimble,' and they went shopping. Grimble's idea of shopping was to go into a shop, find something he wanted, and say, 'I'll buy it.' Mrs Grimble did not work like that. She went into a shop, found something she liked and then spent the next half hour looking at a lot of things similar to it, that she didn't mind, to make sure she liked the first thing she had seen as much as she thought she had liked it when she first saw it. This wasted a lot of time and was very weary for their feet.

After his mother had bought a few womanish things made out of buckles and elastic they went into a food shop. Grimble headed straight for the turkey counter and looked with interest at the turkeys. His mother bought lemons. So Grimble, watching his mother out of the corner of his eye, stood in front of the Christmas puddings and as Mrs Grimble moved off to the tomato ketchup shelf he said, 'Oh look ... Christmas puddings for small families. What a good idea. I thought you could only buy enormous ones.'

'Heavy things Christmas puddings,' said his mother. 'Make you feel very tired – like eating hedgehogs. You go and wait for me at the launderette.'

CHRISTMAS PUDDINGS FOR SMALL FAMILIES

Grimble left his mother in the food store and went to the launderette and watched the clothes go round. It was a bit like colour television only even less plot.

He was just getting interested in a green shirt which was twisting itself affectionately around a pair of white underpants, when his mother came in with a large parcel and said, 'Come ON Grimble, let's go home.'

Grimble took one corner of the parcel and his mother took the other and they carried it home and on the way back he said to his mother, very casually, 'Tell me . . . what would be a good thing to do with three slices of stale toast?' His mother was a very surprising woman. Most mothers would have said, 'throw them away', or else pretend not to have heard; not Mrs Grimble. She put down the parcel, sat on the pavement, and said, 'Three pieces of stale toast. I know exactly what you can do. You can make welsh rarebit with some cheese and an egg and some mustard, if you like mustard, and I shall pay you 2p for every welsh rarebit you make.'

Grimble looked at Mrs Grimble and thought, 'She really is quite a splendid woman. Three times 2p are exactly 6p, which is what I lost on my thin sliced loaf . . . and at home there is a very good book on cooking. It will tell me all about welsh rabbits.'

3. Four Shopping Days
to Christmas

Now there were only four more proper shopping days to Christmas. Father Grimble was in the study looking at some very small islands on the globe through his microscope . . . which is a machine that makes small things look bigger. Mother Grimble was in bed with her feet and Grimble was on holiday. That morning he had had his first proper holiday feeling; first he did not get up and then he quite especially did not go to school and at nine o'clock there was no roll call, and he didn't answer his name. He purposely did not have milk at eleven, although he would have quite liked a glass, and then they had lunch.

Grimble cooked. A bag of potato crisps, peanut-butter sandwiches with chutney, a tin of baked beans, a $2\frac{1}{2}$p piece of fudge and a bottle of fizzy lemonade with two straws. Grimble did not understand how anyone drank out of a lemonade bottle with less than two straws and as straws are very cheap – eighty-three straws cost the same as a bottle of lemonade – it was just meanness when people gave you a single one.

The best thing about Grimble's lunch was the washing up. There was hardly any, and he left it for his mother to do when she felt better.

A very odd thing happened after lunch. You know how you can go weeks and weeks without getting a letter and then suddenly get two? Well, after lunch the postman came and there were three letters, all for Grimble. Three letters – although one was in a brown envelope.

He took them up to his bedroom and opened them carefully. The first was from his Aunt Percy. He knew because she had funny handwriting with words underlined.

As he opened it he thought he noticed a one pound note lurking just inside the flap, but he read the letter first . . .

Dear Grimble, here is one pound for Christmas. I shall take cat away to the sea for a few days. We shall probably go by bus.
Your loving
Aunt Persimmon

He took out his notebook, in which there was a

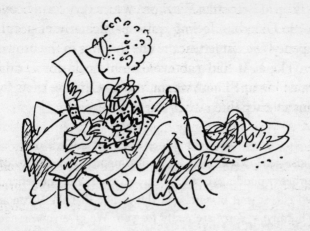

page at the end headed CASH, and crossed out 19p and wrote 119p; then he thought I have not been very clever and he rubbed out the 119 and put a 1 in front of the 19. There. One should be able to get a jolly decent Christmas tree for 119p AND have a bit left over for some washing up powder, which was going to be his Christmas present for his mother.

The second letter was from David Sebastian Waghorn.

Dear Grimble,

Will you come and spend the day with us on Thursday. If we do not hear from you, I shall expect you after breakfast. If you cannot come, come after breakfast and explain why. DSW.

David Sebastian Waghorn WAS a very funny boy.

So Grimble, feeling quite particularly cheerful, opened the last letter; the one that was in the brown envelope. It had not even been stuck down, and said: 'Dear Sir or Madam,' which Grimble thought not a very polite way to start a letter.

You are probably going to get very fat at Christmas. All those rich foods washed down with important wine followed by heavy puddings covered in cream and brandy butter and old cheese and biscuits and things like that. Well, we at Thumpyew Farm are ready for you. We give you orange juice and hot water flavoured with just a teeny bit of lemon and on Sundays you get two peeled grapes, and in hardly any time at all you will regain your youth and your health and your figure. Just think about it as you stuff roast turkey into yourself next week. We at Thumpyew are ready and willing to help YOU get THIN ...

and it gave an address to which one could reply.

Now I wonder why they chose me, thought Grimble. He opened the door of a cupboard that had a mirror attached to it and stood in front of it, sideways with his shirt tucked under his chin. Well, his back was certainly thinner than his tummy. I mean his back sort of caved in while his tummy stuck out, but surely not as far as that. Anyway how did Thumpyew know he was going to stuff himself with turkey and things. Unless he did something about it, the chances were that on Christmas Day he was going to get fishfingers.

He put the pound note into his wallet slipped the three letters under his pillow and went out. In the shopping street there was a greengrocer called Flewett who sold Christmas trees. A Christmas tree, Grimble decided, was absolutely completely essential to Christmas, and he stood in front of the shop looking at a notice which said 20p a foot. He was just wondering what people could do with an extra foot (win a 3-legged race by oneself?) when he realized that it did not mean a foot with five toes at the end and a shoe on the outside, but a foot with twelve inches to it.

So for 80p he could buy a four-foot tree, and as he had 119p he would still have 39p left to buy something for 40p with 1p off for his mother. He peered through the shop window and saw someone peering out at him and he waved; and the person who was looking out waved, so he smiled and the person smiled back. It was a boy with glasses and freckles and suddenly he recognized him. It was a boy from his class. He looked closely at him and said, 'Grimble' (for it was he) 'you are definitely getting a little fat.' Thumpyew was right. 'Now that you are on holiday you are not taking enough exercise', and he started hopping around outside the shop, watching himself in the shop window and wondering whether he was suddenly going to get thinner or whether it took a long time.

As he was hopping around the greengrocer came out and said, 'Excuse me, are you all right?' Grimble said, 'Yes. I'm just taking a little exercise.' Mr Flewett looked at him and said, 'If it's exercise you want you can do some delivering for me; Christmas trees; I pay according to the length of tree. You look a good strong boy. You can take this three foot tree to station-master Wheeler at the station for 5p.'

'Oh thank you,' said Grimble. 'I know Mr Wheeler,' and he took the tree and went off to the station.

He found that the best way of carrying the tree was folding his hands in front of his tummy, getting Mr Flewett to put the trunk into them, and resting the top of the tree against his head. It was quite easy to carry that way, although people in the street thought he was a Christmas tree on legs and some of them ran to the other side of the road.

Mr Wheeler was very pleased to see Grimble with

his tree and gave him a free platform ticket and they went on to the platform and there was a weighing machine. 'I wonder,' Grimble asked, 'whether I might weigh myself on your machine?' Mr Wheeler said, 'Yes of course you can, and you need not put in a penny. I have the key,' and he opened up the machine at the back and pressed a lever. There was a click and Grimble stood on the machine and he weighed just under five stone. As he got off the machine a card popped out of a slot and it had:

YOUR FORTUNE

written on it. His fortune was a small card with printing:

BEWARE OF STRANGERS WITH BLACK HAIR. YOU ARE GOING ON A JOURNEY. THIS IS A GOOD TIME FOR LOVE. MONEY WILL BE DIFFICULT TO FIND.

'I don't know any strangers with black hair,' said Grimble, 'What very peculiar advice.' Mr Wheeler said the machine was very old and it only had two fortunes. The other said:

A HAPPY EVENT WILL TAKE PLACE SOON.

SOMEONE YOU LOVE IS GOING ON A JOURNEY.
BE VERY CAREFUL NOT TO GET TOO CLOSE TO
WATER.

'That means if I weighed myself twice I would
get both fortunes.'

'That's right,' said the station-master. 'We like
people to do that because of the "journey" part.
That way more people go on the railway.'

Grimble went back to the shop and realized that
he now had enough money to buy a six-foot tree
. . . if he didn't get any soap powder for his mother.
A six-foot tree would be marvellous. Six foot was
much bigger than he was. When he got back to the
greengrocer, he decided to ask whether he might
buy a tree for himself with a bit off the price for
delivering it to himself, but as soon as Mr Flewett
saw him he said, 'Here you are. Take this four
footer to Number 26, The Terrace; they've got a
children's party with dancing-round-the-tree, and
the tree isn't there yet.' So Grimble took the tree
and ran.

It was very heavy, but as he waddled along he
said to himself, 'Now we'll be able to get the biggest
Christmas tree anywhere, especially if I get a
special price for delivering my own tree.'

When he got back there was only one tree left outside the shop. It was the biggest one of all and the greengrocer was waiting for Grimble and said, 'That's my last tree; we'll have to take it between us because it's too big for one person to carry.' Grimble said, 'All right ... but will there be no more trees?'

'Not now,' said Mr Flewett. 'Trees are all finished now. We start selling tangerines after this.'

Grimble was very sad. He liked tangerines but you can't put presents under a tangerine. You can't even put a lot of candles into a tangerine and light them. And there was not another Christmas-tree shop in the district. 'Come on then,' said the greengrocer, and he took the thick end and led the way. Grimble got hold of the trunk near the top and followed him down the street. It must have looked funny. The big greengrocer at the front end – and all you could see at the back was a pair of shoes under a lot of branches. 'I can't see where I'm going,' shouted Grimble towards the trunk.

'You just hold your end up,' shouted the greengrocer over his shoulder. 'I'll pull you in the right direction.'

They walked a very long way and then he heard the man say, 'Here we are, hold on,' and he heard

the trunk drop and a bell ring and a woman's voice saying, 'Oh there it is, you'd better hide it in the shed in the garden because I don't want someone to see it just yet.'

Grimble thought it was rather a nice voice, a bit like his mother's, and then the voice said, 'Will you put it on my account please,' and Mr Flewett said, 'Certainly Madam, good-bye,' and the lady went back into the house and Grimble came out from the tree and looked up and it was his house. He had delivered the Christmas tree to his own house.

He helped Mr Flewett hide the tree in the shed and then he walked about for a few minutes – thinking. First he thought he must have managed to lose a little weight after all that exercise and that delivering Christmas trees was better than living on nothing but orange juice and peeled grapes.

And then he thought about his mother. She had said she didn't want 'someone' to see the Christmas tree and the only someone he could think of was himself. He decided he would pretend not to know about the tree so she wouldn't be upset. Really he was very pleased – it was one less thing for him to organize.

Then he went inside. 'There you are,' said his mother. 'Did you have a nice day?' 'Yes thank you,' said Grimble. 'Are your feet better?' His mother said they were a bit better but she was going to bed and if it was not too much trouble could she have some fudge.

As Grimble had never made fudge, he said that might take a little time, but his mother said that didn't matter. 'I have plenty of time now because there is nothing else to do, is there?'

'I hope not,' said Grimble and went off to find a book called *How to Make Fudge and Other Good Tricks*.

4. David Sebastian Waghorn

IT was now Thursday and Grimble had arranged to spend the day with his friend David Sebastian Waghorn. The Waghorns lived in a large house, which was built a very short time ago but tried to look old.

Mr Waghorn was a loud man who shouted a lot. The odd thing was that he did not only shout when he was angry, the way most people do; he shouted all the time.

'HELLO GRIMBLE,' he shouted. 'HERE'S GRIMBLE,' and then he raised his voice and shouted, 'GRIMBLE IS HERE.'

So Grimble said, 'Good morning Mr Waghorn. I am here.'

'RECOGNIZED YOU,' shouted Mr Waghorn, 'KNEW WHO YOU WERE. MUST GO TO WORK. GOOD-BYE,' and then in case everyone had not heard him he shouted it again: 'GOOD-BYE.'

Mrs Waghorn was a small quiet lady with blue hair. Not bright blue but a pastel shade, which some hairdressers think is nice. She was very kind to people, to make up for her husband shouting so loudly.

Mrs Waghorn liked washing up better than anything and, when Grimble and David Sebastian Waghorn had stood for a minute or two whispering to each other, she put on some rubber gloves and went off to do the dishes with a lovely smile on her face.

Grimble and David Sebastian Waghorn went off to the sitting room to inspect a new book called 'Party Tricks', which Mr Waghorn had given his

son as a non-birthday present. They lay on the floor and started to look for something which, the book promised, would 'confuse and delight friends and family'.

One of the best tricks in the book was: take a pack of cards which everyone will think is a real pack, but only you know that all the cards are queens of spades. Ask someone to pick a card, to look at it and put it back into the pack; then shuffle the cards, pretend to examine them carefully and take one from the pack. Naturally this will be the queen of spades. People will think you very clever.

'I wonder how often you can play that trick on the same person,' Grimble said. 'After you have shown someone a different queen of spades half a dozen times, I think they could get suspicious . . .'

'You know something,' said Grimble. 'There are fifty-two different cards in the pack. Suppose they are not all queens of spades but just ordinary cards and you went up to fifty-two different people and said, TAKE A CARD. PUT IT BACK. IT WAS THE QUEEN OF SPADES. Unless you are terribly unlucky at least one of them will have taken the queen of spades and be very impressed and those who took one of the other queens will be fairly impressed. The rest of the people won't be very impressed. Do you think that is a good trick?'

'No,' said David Sebastian Waghorn. 'Actually the best sort of trick is when there are two of 'us' against one of 'them'. Suppose I give my mother a pack of cards from which she picks one and puts it back. You could be standing behind her as she looks at it and then you can signal to me and tell me what card she took.'

'That is a very good idea indeed,' said Grimble.

'If we worked hard on that we could go into business together as Grimble and Waghorn, Conjurers to the Nobility; and if things went well and we learnt more than one trick we might appear on a Royal Variety Programme and be By Appointment Grimble and Waghorn.'

'Or Waghorn and Grimble sounds quite nice,' suggested David Sebastian Waghorn.

'I was taking the names in alphabetical order,' said Grimble. 'G comes before W.'

'All right,' said David Sebastian Waghorn, 'let's practise our trick.'

'Cards are either spades, hearts, diamonds or clubs – so when you see which card has been taken you signal; S is for spades and shirt so you point to your shirt. C is for clubs and collar. H is for heart and hair and D is for diamonds and ... and ... dustbin?'

'How are we going to find a dustbin?' asked Grimble.

'A very sensible remark,' said David Sebastian Waghorn.

'What else begins with a D?'

After quite a lot of discussion they decided David Sebastian Waghorn began with a D, and if Grimble did the signalling he should point to David and if David did it he should point to himself, only be sure not to point to his hair, collar or shirt or the trick would go wrong.

When it came to actual cards, they decided to hold up fingers for the numbered cards – ace to ten and hold up the right fist for jack, the left fist for queen and both fists for king. They practised the trick for quite a long time before going into the kitchen to try it on Mrs Waghorn.

'I say,' began Grimble, 'I wonder whether you would like us to show you rather a clever trick.'

Mrs Waghorn said she would like to see it, especially if she could do it without taking her washing-up gloves off.

'Well,' said Grimble, 'they are your cards but the trick would go better with bare hands.'

So Mrs Waghorn took off her gloves and David Sebastian stood behind her and Grimble held out the pack and said, 'Take a card. Look at it. Put it back. Now,' said Grimble, 'I am going to tell you what card it was.'

David Sebastian Waghorn started signalling furiously. First he touched his nose, then he held up his right fist, then suddenly he changed his mind, pulled down his right fist and held up his left

fist, and his mother turned around and said. 'If you are going to hit me I shall be very angry and tell your father and you know what he will do.'

'Shout,' said David Sebastian Waghorn, quietly.

'Now,' said Grimble, 'let me tell you which card you picked. It was without very much shadow of doubt the queen of diamonds. Thank you, thank you, thank you.'

'Oh dear,' said Mrs Waghorn, 'I seem to think it was the nine of spades but with all those wavings from David it is very hard to concentrate. Why don't you two boys go out into the garden with a football?' And the two boys went out in the garden with a football. David Sebastian Waghorn was very angry, 'The trouble about my mother is that she has no card sense. It WAS the queen of diamonds.'

Grimble thought they ought to forget about card tricks for the moment and start on football.

They began by putting down their jackets as goal-posts and playing on the same side and every time they scored a goal they hugged each other the way footballers do on television. As there were no goalkeepers they scored a lot of goals and there was more hugging than football so they gave up and went back into the house and played psychiatrists; these are a special kind of doctor who do a lot of talking.

Grimble lay on the couch and David Sebastian Waghorn sat in a chair and said 'Tell me now Mr ... err ... Grimble did you say your name was ... what appears to be the matter?'

'It's Christmas ...' said Grimble. 'I have got a cake and my mother has bought a heavy parcel and there is a Christmas tree hidden in the shed and I can do a pretty pathetic conjuring trick and is it going to be enough?'

'What do you expect from this – Christmas I think you call it, Mr err Grimble?'

'Well,' said Grimble, 'I expect rather a lot. Like a brown Windsor soup or at least a fairly brown

Windsor soup. And then turkey and everything and Christmas pudding and things and crackers and balloons and all that. And a cake but I've got the cake.'

David Sebastian Waghorn looked very serious and said, 'You are suffering from Christmasitis and if you are not careful you will get Christmeasles and may have to have a Christmasectomy. I suggest you go into the garden and try to score a goal using your right foot. That will be seven pounds and fifty-five pence.'

'There is another thing I'm worried about,' said Grimble. 'I do not have as much money as I would like to have.'

'That,' said David Sebastian Waghorn, 'is much more serious. In fact I do not know when I heard of a more serious disease. Do your parents talk a lot about money?'

'No,' said Grimble, 'hardly ever.'

'Then they have enough,' said David. 'Can you come back next week?'

'I could,' said Grimble, 'but it may be too late.'

For lunch they had lamb chops cooked in bread-crumbs and spinach with mashed potatoes and then a chocolate pudding and in the afternoon Mrs Waghorn took them to the cinema and for all that time Grimble completely forgot about Christmas.

But after tea Grimble began thinking again and had another look at the party trick book. Christmas had quite long gaps between meals and if there was nothing organized, which the old Grimbles were very good at . . . I mean the old Grimbles were very good at not being organized, then it was up to Grimble to provide the entertainment.

There was quite a good trick in which you tucked

a penny between your fingers and opened out your hand, and no one saw anything and then suddenly you had a penny in your hand. Grimble tried that trick a lot but finally the penny, which kept falling on the floor, rolled under the sofa, and he gave up.

Grimble left before Mr Waghorn came home – he decided he wasn't feeling strong enough to be shouted at – and when he got to his house he decided he needed something strengthening to eat, like fudge.

The night before, in his Fudge Book, he had read that you can make fudge of any flavour you like. Now onion was a flavour Grimble liked very much and he was sure it was strengthening. Onion fudge. The words had a sort of rightness about them. Onion fudge ... like strawberry jam or bacon sandwich.

Grimble put a saucepan on to the stove and then he found an onion and cut it in half and put it in the pan and then he went to look for some condensed milk. There was none in the larder and he couldn't find any in his father's study or in the bathroom where his mother might have left it – she used amazing things, like eggs, for washing her hair. Anyway there was no milk anywhere, but quite an interesting smell was coming from the kitchen.

He looked round and found it was coming from the saucepan ... so he took it from the flame and when it was a bit cool he noticed that the onion had stuck to the bottom of the pan, because of the heat. By far the best way to unstick things that have burnt on to pans is to pour on some water ... so when the pan had cooled down he poured on some water and let it boil until the burnt onion was loose and then, just before he threw away the water, he decided to taste it . . . he poured it into a cup, blew on it to make sure it was cool, and took a sip. It was not just golden coloured water. It was very good onion soup . . . especially when he had added some salt to it.

5. The After-soup Announcement

I DON'T suppose, said Grimble to himself, that we need have a very large turkey, but it ought to be a turkey. A pigeon put under his father's microscope might look all right, but he was sure it wouldn't taste the same.

At breakfast his father was in a very good mood. They ate a lot of streaky bacon, which his father

cooked under the grill because that way the fat ran off and the bacon became crisp, and you can eat it with your fingers. Also they read the papers. FATHER CHRISTMAS HITS CHILD IN CHEMIST SHOP said the headline in one of them.

'What on earth was Father Christmas *doing* in a chemist shop?' asked Grimble.

'There are two things,' said his father. 'Either he had a headache and was getting an aspirin, or he was stocking up with talcum powder. Nearly everyone gets talcum powder. It is one of the most giving things there is, so Father Christmas needs a lot of it.'

'Does he make his own?' asked Grimble.

'This is a silly conversation,' said his father. 'What happened to Chelsea?'

'I do not wish to know that,' said Grimble. 'What is happening to Plymouth Argyle?'

They left a very neat pile of washing-up for Mrs Grimble who had gone to bed with her feet again, and Mr Grimble said 'Come into the study . . . I want to talk to you.'

Grimble tucked his shirt, which usually hung outside his trousers, back into his trousers and followed his father into the study. 'Sit down,' said Mr Grimble. It sounded quite an important meeting, so Grimble rubbed his shoes against the back of his socks to polish them and sat down.

'Well now,' said his father, 'I have news for you. Next Wednesday is Christmas Day.'

'I know that,' said Grimble. 'I have known that all winter.'

'Please let me continue. Next Wednesday is Christmas Day and today we are going to go to a restaurant for lunch. Do you understand?'

Grimble said he understood both things his father had said. But even if they went to the best restaurant anywhere and ate everything that restaurant sold, he would still be very hungry by next Wednesday. Unlike camels, who had a drink and could make it last for a week, human beings had to be fed daily.

'At this luncheon,' said his father, ignoring Grimble, 'I shall make an important announcement concerning the whole Grimble family and Christmas.'

'Isn't it possible to tell me what it is now?' asked Grimble. 'You see I have been worrying quite a lot about Christmas and lunchtime is still hours away.'

His father shook his head. 'All I can tell you is that the news will be announced directly after the soup.'

'Suppose we have grapefruit instead?' asked Grimble.

'No soup, no news,' said his father and started twisting the globe of the world. 'Second time today

I have lost the Falkland Islands,' he muttered. 'Ah there they are. Just to the right of Patagonia,' and he got a magnifying glass and examined them carefully.

Grimble went out partly happy because he liked restaurants but partly worried because he did like to know exactly what was going to happen, when it was going to happen . . . and an important family announcement after the soup was a bit too vague for comfort. Grimble found his encyclopedia and looked up turkey. 'Turkey' . . . said the book: 'Republican country lying partly in Asia and partly in Europe.' As this was not the turkey he had in mind he looked up the next column and it said: 'Turkey – large game bird with a pendent dilatable appendage on the head and a wrinkled and tuberculed neck. The male weighs up to 34 pounds.' He did not understand that – except the weight part.

As the encyclopedia did not give the price, he went down the street to the butcher's shop, where there were a lot of turkeys in the window with THIS JOINT cards stuck into them and every THIS JOINT card had a price written on it.

The small turkeys cost at least two pounds 50p and some of the bigger ones cost much more than that. For a boy who had 119p, some tree delivery money, and an Irish 5p piece it was quite obvious that this was too expensive. With a swift decision such as Nelson, Napoleon and other leaders have had to make in their time, Grimble made up his mind: NO TURKEY FROM ME TO THE OLD GRIMBLES. They cost too much and it's not really my job . . . anyway the announcement after the soup might well make the whole idea of turkey-buying unnecessary.

On the other hand . . . on the other hand I have five fingers . . . that was David Sebastian Waghorn's joke . . . (David Sebastian Waghorn was a very funny boy.)

On the other hand he had not yet bought any real Christmas presents for his parents – the fudge he had made for them was all right but he had used THEIR sugar and THEIR milk and THEIR chocolate so it was really more their present to them.

119p is a fair amount of money to spend on presents for two people so perhaps he could keep his earnings from the Christmas trees for himself. He thought about it and decided he should spend 79p on his father and 40p on his mother. Then he thought that was a bit mean; his mother had been very good to him about the welsh rarebits, so he made it 69 and 50. His mother ought to have something for her feet and his father some arrows that would stick to the globe, so that he could find places again when he was looking for them.

He went into a stationer's shop and there were some good red stick-on arrows in an envelope that cost 19p, and as this left exactly 50p and the shop sold a book called GRIMBLE by Clement Freud for

25p, he bought two. He thought it was a jolly good name for a book.

For his mother he bought four 12½p tins of talcum powder, one smelling of lavender, one of violets, one of roses and one of French fern. They did not have any onion talcum powder. He asked and the chemist said not.

Back in the Grimble household, preparations for going out to the restaurant were in full swing. Mr Grimble had put a dust sheet over his globe, combed his hair, and put on a pair of purple socks. As neither of the Grimbles drove a car (in fact the Grimbles did not have a car) a taxi had been ordered to take them to the bus stop. It was going to be a really proper outing.

The restaurant to which the Grimbles went was called The French Restaurant. All the waiters were Italian and the *chef* was Indian. He sometimes came in and watched people eat to make sure they did not leave anything on their plates, and when they had finished he would turn to the waiters and say, 'There, I was right.'

A man with a long finger came up to the Grimbles and said, 'Follow my finger,' and he held it up and they followed it to a table. Then the man gave them a menu and went away.

After a while he came back with a piece of paper and a pencil, to write down what they had chosen to eat. Grimble ordered vegetable soup and some roast chicken and bacon and fried onion and spinach. His parents said prawn cocktail and duck, both of them. He thought that was a waste. If they were both going to have the same things, they could have had it at home. Restaurants were for being different in.

When he had finished his soup and his father had finally got hold of the last prawn in the cocktail glass and swallowed it, he gave a small cough and said, 'Here is the Christmas announcement. At half past three tomorrow afternoon the Grimble household will leave for Africa by taxi and bus and then by train and boat. We shall spend Christmas on the SS *Particular*, which is a very luxurious kind of passenger ship with nine out of ten for roast turkey and the best Christmas-pudding maker in the Mediterranean Sea. I expect you have heard of Particular Christmas pudding.'

'On Boxing Day we arrive in Ifni, which is at the top end of the Sahara desert and we will take sand samples, which I need very badly for my work. We will then fly home.'

'In an aeroplane?' asked Grimble.

'I have always felt that to be the best way to fly,' said his father.

The chicken and the duck then arrived and the waiter got all the vegetables wrong.

'It is going to be an absolutely marvellous Christmas,' said Grimble. 'It is going to be the best Christmas I have ever had, I know it is.'

'There are,' said his father, 'one or two things I feel I should tell you. While the good ship *Particular*'s chef is a master in the art of making Christmas puddings he has absolutely no idea about the manufacture of a Christmas cake. I should have bought a Christmas cake and taken it with us – but I regret that it is now too late. It is very sad, but I only thought about this on the bus.'

Grimble turned a bit red and said, 'It so happens that I have a Christmas cake ready and iced and rather looking forward to going to Africa.'

His parents looked at him with great admiration.

'It also happens,' said Grimble, 'that my presents to you are very small and light and they will be most suitable to be brought back on an aeroplane.'

They munched their chicken and duck and as the old Grimbles picked up their pieces of duck in their fingers, Grimble realized that this would be an all right thing to do ; after all it was a *French* restaurant.

When he had pulled the wishbone with his father . . . and lost – his father was very pleased – he said to his mother, 'If we are going to Africa, why did you buy a Christmas tree?'

'Against burglars,' said his mother. 'If a burglar sees a Christmas tree in a house he knows there is someone in and does not burgle anything.'

'Why did you hide the tree in the shed then?'

'Well, we don't want the burglars to know everything,' said his mother.

'And the cardboard box,' said Grimble, 'the one we brought home from the shops. What was in that?'

'Washing powder,' said his mother, '2p off.'

Grimble ordered ice cream, but as he had eaten too much soup and chicken and onions he could not finish the ice cream, and the Italian waiter said, 'As it is very near Christmas I will give you some ice cream and you can take it home in a box and have it for tea.'

It really was going to be a super Christmas.

WOOF! *Allan Ahlberg*

Eric is a perfectly ordinary boy. Perfectly ordinary that is, until the night when, safely tucked up in bed, he slowly but surely turns into a dog! Fritz Wagner's drawings illustrate this funny and exciting story superbly.

VERA PRATT AND THE FALSE MOUSTACHES *Brough Girling*

There were times when Wally Pratt wished his mum was more ordinary and not the fanatic mechanic she was, but when he and his friends find themselves caught up in a real 'cops and robbers' affair, he is more than glad to have his mum, Vera, to help them.

SADDLEBOTTOM *Dick King-Smith*

Hilarious adventures of a Wessex Saddleback pig whose white saddle is in the wrong place, to the chagrin of his mother.

SLADE *John Tully*

Slade has a mission – to investigate life on Earth. When Eddie discovers the truth about Slade he gets a whole lot more adventure than he bargained for.

A TASTE OF BLACKBERRIES
Doris Buchanan Smith

The moving story about a young boy who has to come to terms with the tragic death of his best friend and the guilty feeling that he could somehow have saved him.

THE PRIME MINISTER'S BRAIN *Gillian Cross*

The fiendish Demon Headmaster plans to gain control of No. 10 Downing Street and lure the Prime Minister into his evil clutches.

JASON BODGER AND
THE PRIORY GHOST *Gene Kemp*

A ghost story, both funny and exciting, about Jason, the bane of every teacher's life, who is pursued by the ghost of a little nun from the twelfth century!

HALFWAY ACROSS THE GALAXY AND
TURN LEFT *Robin Klein*

A humorous account of what happens to a family banished from their planet Zygron, when they have to spend a period of exile on Earth.

SUPER GRAN TO THE RESCUE *Forrest Wilson*

The punchpacking, baddiebiffing escapades of the world's No. 1 senior citizen superhero – Super Gran! Now a devastating series on ITV!

TOM TIDDLER'S GROUND
John Rowe Townsend

Vic and Brain are given an old rowing boat which leads to the unravelling of a mystery and a happy reunion of two friends. An exciting adventure story.

THE FINDING *Nina Bawden*

Alex doesn't know his birthday because he was found abandoned next to Cleopatra's Needle, so instead of a birthday he celebrates his Finding. After inheriting an unexpected fortune, Alex's life suddenly becomes very exciting indeed.

RACSO AND THE RATS OF NIMH
Jane Leslie Conly

When fieldmouse Timothy Frisby rescues young Racso, the city rat, from drowning it's the beginning of a friendship and an adventure. The two are caught up in the struggle of the Rats of NIMH to save their home from destruction. A powerful sequel to MRS FRISBY AND THE RATS OF NIMH.

NICOBOBINUS *Terry Jones*

Nicobobinus and his friend, Rosie, find themselves in all sorts of intriguing adventures when they set out to find the Land of the Dragons long ago. Stunningly illustrated by Michael Foreman.

FRYING AS USUAL *Joan Lingard*

When Mr Francetti breaks his leg it looks as if his fish restaurant will have to close so Tony, Rosita and Paula decide to keep things going.

DRIFT *William Mayne*

A thrilling adventure of a young boy and an Indian girl, stranded on a frozen floating island in the North American wilderness.

JELLYBEAN *Tessa Duder*

A sensitive modern novel about Geraldine, alias 'Jellybean', who leads a rather solitary life as the only child of a single parent. She's tired of having to fit in with her mother's busy schedule, but a new friend and a performance of 'The Nutcracker Suite' change everything.

THE PRIESTS OF FERRIS *Maurice Gee*

Susan Ferris and her cousin Nick return to the world of O which they had saved from the evil Halfmen, only to find that O is now ruled by cruel and ruthless priests. Can they save the inhabitants of O from tyranny? An action-packed and gripping story by the author of prize-winning THE HALFMEN OF O.

THE SEA IS SINGING *Rosalind Kerven*

In her seaside Shetland home, Tess is torn between the plight of the whales and loyalty to her father and his job on the oil rig. A haunting and thought-provoking novel.

BACK HOME *Michelle Magorian*

A marvellously gripping story of an irrepressible girl's struggle to adjust to a new life. Twelve-year-old Rusty, who had been evacuated to the United States when she was seven, returns to the grey austerity of post-war Britain.

THE BEAST MASTER *Andre Norton*

Spine-chilling science fiction – treachery and revenge! Hosteen Storm is a man with a mission to find and punish Brad Quade, the man who killed his father long ago on Terra, the planet where life no longer exists.

COME BACK SOON *Judy Gardiner*

Val's family seem quite an odd bunch and their life is hectic but happy. But then Val's mother walks out on them and Val's carefree life is suddenly quite different. This is a moving but funny story.

AMY'S EYES *Richard Kennedy*

When a doll changes into a man it means that anything might happen . . . and in this magical story all kinds of strange and wonderful things do happen to Amy and her sailor doll, the Captain. Together they set off on a fantastic journey on a quest for treasure more valuable than mere gold.

ASTERCOTE *Penelope Lively*

Astercote village was destroyed by plague in the fourteenth century and Mair and her brother Peter find themselves caught up in a strange adventure when an ancient superstition is resurrected.

THE HOUNDS OF THE MÓRRÍGAN
Pat O'Shea

When the Great Queen Mórrígan, evil creature from the world of Irish mythology, returns to destroy the world, Pidge and Brigit are the children chosen to thwart her. How they go about it makes an hilarious, moving story, full of original and unforgettable characters.

COME SING, JIMMY JO *Katherine Paterson*

An absorbing story about eleven-year-old Jimmy Jo's rise to stardom, and the problem of coping with fame.